Horace and Morris Join the Chorus
(but what about Dolores?)

For Moustro Brian Hall
—J. H.

To my brothers, Michael and Mark . . .
"The Zucchini Brothers"
—A. W.

ALADDIN PAPERBACKS
An imprint of Simon & Schuster Children's Publishing Division
1230 Avenue of the Americas, New York, NY 10020
Text copyright © 2002 by James Howe
Illustrations copyright © 2002 by Amy Walrod
All rights reserved, including the right of reproduction in whole or in part in any form.
ALADDIN PAPERBACKS and colophon are registered trademarks of Simon & Schuster, Inc.
Also available in an Atheneum Books for Young Readers hardcover edition.
Designed by Abelardo Martínez
The text of this book was set in Gararond.
The illustrations for this book were rendered in acrylic on paper.
Manufactured in China
First Aladdin Paperbacks edition November 2005
4 6 8 10 9 7 5
The Library of Congress has cataloged the hardcover edition as follows:
Howe, James, 1946-
Horace and Morris join the chorus (but what about Dolores?) / written by James Howe;
illustrated by Amy Walrod.—1st ed.
p. cm.
Summary: Dolores is upset when her friends are chosen to sing in the chorus,
but she finds a way to become part of the performance.
ISBN 0-689-83939-1 (hc.)
[1. Mice—Fiction 2. Singing—Fiction.] I. Walrod, Amy, ill. II. Title
PZ7.H83727 Hmg 2001
[E]—dc12   00-040151
ISBN-13: 978-1-4169-0616-2 (pbk.)
ISBN-10: 1-4169-0616-9 (pbk.)
1209 SCP

Horace and Morris Join the Chorus
(but what about Dolores?)

LALALAA...

written by JAMES HOWE

illustrated by AMY WALROD

ALADDIN PAPERBACKS
New York London Toronto Sydney

Horace and Morris but mostly Dolores loved to sing.

Horace sang the high notes.

Morris sang the low notes.

One day . . .

"A chorus!" Dolores cried. "I've always wanted to sing
in a chorus. And now we can sing in one together!"

"Welcome!" Moustro Provolone boomed.

"Please come right in and let me hear you sing."

Horace sang "Squeak to Me Softly of Love." He poured his heart and soul into the high notes.

"What clarity, what vibrato!" Moustro Provolone exclaimed, clasping his paws to his heart.

Morris sang "Somewhere Under the Rainspout." His voice caressed the low notes.

"What pitch, what pathos!" Moustro Provolone cried, wiping a tear from his eye.

Finally, it was Dolores's turn.

Dolores sang "The Mouse in the Wheel Goes Round and Round." She bellowed out notes no one had ever heard before.

THE MOUSE IN THE WHEEL GOES ROUND AND ROUND...

"What . . . what enthusiasm!" Moustro Provolone uttered, lowering his paws from his ears.

"He loved us!"

Dolores assured her friends.

"We're in!"

But later that day, when they went to see who had been accepted into the chorus . . .

There were the names of Horace and Morris . . . but not Dolores.

"There must be a mistake!"

"I'll go talk to Moustro Provolone."

"I'm sorry, Dolores," Moustro Provolone said. He had a sad look on his face as if he had just eaten blue cheese. "You're very enthusiastic, but I'm afraid your singing is just a little too . . . loud."

"I can sing softly," Dolores said.

Moustro Provolone began to squirm as if he'd just eaten *bad* blue cheese. "It isn't only that, Dolores. I'm afraid you just don't have an ear for music."

"Of course I do!" Dolores shouted. "I have two of them!"

Dolores stomped off in a huff.

Every day, Horace and Morris passed Dolores on their way to rehearsals for the big concert.

Dolores tried not to feel hurt. She tried not to feel angry. But in the end, she felt both those things and something more. She felt sorry for herself.

"This is not like me at all!" she declared. "I've got to find something else to do."

She knew her friend
Chloris was in the chorus,
but what about Boris?

"I'm on my way to band
rehearsal," Boris told her.
"It's too bad you don't
play an instrument,
Dolores. Then you could
be in the band. But at
least you'll be in the
audience. The audience
is important too."

Determined not to feel
sorry for herself any longer,
Dolores went exploring.

But when she called out, "Hey, you guys, look
what I found!" there was no one there to come
running and call back, "What is it, Dolores?"

So she tried climbing a tree. But when she got to the top, she felt lonelier and sorrier for herself than ever.

"I've had it!" Dolores said. "I'm going to write Moustro Provolone a letter."

Dear Moustro Provolone,

I love to sing more than anything. It makes me feel good inside. When I'm told I can't sing, the words really sting — and my heart hurts as much as my pride.

Who tells a bird she shouldn't be heard? Singing is just what birds do! So please take my word — I'm a lot like a bird. I have to sing out loud and true!

Please, Moustro Provolone, doesn't your chorus have a place for Dolores?

Sincerely,
Dolores (the bird)

Dolores felt much better. She slipped the letter under Moustro Provolone's door and skipped away.

The next day . . .

"What rhyme, what rhythm!" Moustro Provolone declared, waving Dolores's letter over his head.

Dolores beamed.

"You are a real poet!" Moustro Provolone went on. "And this would make a great song! May I put it to music for the chorus to sing?"

"Yes!" Dolores exclaimed. "But . . . but . . . what about me?"

"You? Well, of course you must be in the chorus to sing it. It is *your* song! You're right, Dolores, *everyone* has a place in the chorus. Some singers just need a little more help. Will you let me work with you?"

"You bet I will!" Dolores cried.

And so . . .

The night of the big concert, everyone was there.

Chloris and Boris and Horace and Morris . . .
but mostly Dolores.

Horace sang the high notes.
Morris sang the low notes.

And *most* of the time,
Dolores sang notes
everyone had heard before.